DEDICATION

For the Jabrans, Fezzis and Jabirs out there.

JABRAN THE BULLY

Novid Shaid

ISBN: **978-0993044861**

I

Jabran was a dreadful bully. Towering and built like an oak tree, he was awesome and terrifying. Children dared not look into his dark, unfriendly eyes and would run when they heard him stomping by. To top it off, his hair was shoe-polish black, extremely thick and bushy, and gave him the appearance of a wild and hungry cave man. When he was amused, he roared instead of laughed, like this:

"RAAAAAR!"

And when he was irritated, he bellowed instead of shouted, something like this:

"You what? YOOU What? YOOOU WHAAAAT!!"

Jabran had an ugly reputation and did as he pleased. He hung boys upside-down, growled at teachers, challenged grown-ups, chased after cats, sneered at dogs, shook trees and made birds homeless. But the list didn't stop there: he had snatched and gobbled down pack lunches; he had kidnapped boys and removed their trainers; hijacked bicycles; grabbed and sold mobile phones. And he had destroyed things too: pictures, school projects, model aeroplanes, bird cages, school bags, pencil cases, school windows; so far, Jabran had left a trail of misery and destruction.

And no child would ever get him in trouble as they were too afraid of what he might do. Teachers had tried to exclude him; policemen had attempted to charge him, but they could never find anyone brave enough to speak against him.

Once a young lad, little Fezzi, had told on Jabran to the head teacher, Mrs Ali. After Jabran was given a stiff telling-off, he hid in some bushes and waited for the boy after school. Then, as Fezzi came creeping by, Jabran sprang out and pounced on him:

"Been telling on me, have yer? You little weasel?" Said Jabran, grabbing Fezzi by the scruff of the neck, "how about I shake you about a bit?"

Fezzi had been frightened so much that he wet his pants while Jabran laughed in his face and told him worse would happen if Fezzi ever grassed him up again. After that, Jabran forced Fezzi to give him the dessert from his lunch every single day.

Jabran's parents didn't care what he did to make matters worse. His father had been in jail twice and his mother had finally left them some time ago. Jabran's father didn't do much in the house except drink wine, watch television, go on his odd-job runs and sometimes slap Jabran around the house, for Jabran inherited his strength and nastiness from his dad. Jabran never told this to anyone and suffered in silence. However, when the social services came snooping around, Jabran's dad suddenly cleared the house up, hid his alcohol and seemed amiable, warning his son that if he said anything, he would find himself locked in their cellar without food until further notice.

So, you couldn't even complain to Jabran's parents; it seemed there was no hope.

All in all, Jabran was the biggest, meanest eleven-year-old boy you could ever meet. And the people would say there was no hope for him and he was simply a bad apple. He would probably become part of a vicious gang and end up in prison.

However, one day some remarkable things happened, which pleased many people; especially Jabran's victims, which sent shock waves through the town; especially with all the school kids, and finally, a strange thing occurred that some people never found out.

So, what made people laugh and clap was that Jabran broke his leg. What people couldn't comprehend was that Jabran burst into tears and completely changed his ways. And the third thing, the secret, was that Jabran saved the life of a lonely, little soul.

2

The events that led to Jabran's broken leg, his tears and the little soul's freedom were as follows.

It was the beginning of the school holidays and Jabran was free to roam the streets like a hungry wolf and cause more havoc than ever. These days his favourite pastime was terrorising the little boy Fezzi and chasing him around:

"Here, little Fezzi, Wezzi. Come to your master Jabran. Just you wait till I get you, you little rat!"

So, on the very first day of the holidays, Jabran pursued Fezzi all the way through the vast, wooded park and led him into a cul-de-sac.

And, fatefully, at the end of this road, stood the gigantic, ancient, deserted house.

Local people said it was haunted and should be bulldozed. Others said that drug-dealers lurked there, and you would get kidnapped if you went inside. The house had a cramped front garden, which was dominated by immense, overgrown fir trees that stood and swayed before the house like a row of drunken giants, so you couldn't see much of the house from far away. But when you came closer and could see the house behind the trees, it reminded you of a ghostly place you had perhaps seen in a film or read about in a book. Even Jabran feared this place and had never ventured in. Boarded, graffitied bay windows jutted out on two storeys, staring out, like malevolent eyes. A crumbling veranda stood to the left and a set of stone steps led up to the darkened front door. The hipped roof crowned the house, with weather-beaten tiles hanging off the edges, like ghastly earrings. The house had belonged to one of the local gentry and had once held a distinguished position in the town. But now it was an overbearing, unwelcome sight to the locals who were fighting to have it knocked down for new houses.

Therefore, when Fezzi realised where he was being led, and saw the great fir trees and house looming ahead, he stopped running and stood frozen on the spot.

Jabran wasn't far behind and was charging up the road.

"I'm coming to get you my little weasel!" He snarled, now visible to Fezzi on the street.

Jabran was so much bigger than Fezzi that Fezzi's head would hit Jabran's tummy when he stood before him. Or should we say whenever Jabran gripped him in a headlock!

Fezzi peered behind him at the house and then in front of him at the marauding figure of Jabran. If he stayed where he was, Jabran would catch him and smother him in a headlock. He would most probably steal his trainers and make him walk home in his bare feet. But if he tried to escape into the house, who knows what could be waiting for him in there? Drug dealers? Murderers? Even ghosts? And if he did go in, what if Jabran didn't follow? Fezzi would be stuck in this mysterious house all alone and would never see his parents again.

Fezzi could see the delight on Jabran's face now, as those large, dark, remorseless eyes bore into him.

"Ha, ha, ha! I've got you now!" Jabran gasped.

Then Fezzi surmised that Jabran may force him into the house anyway and, after taking deep breath, he ran to the rusty gate, opened it and disappeared behind the enormous fir trees.

Jabran stopped in his tracks instantly and stood there fuming and cursing.

"You stupid little weasel! You little chicken! You watch what I do when I catch you! I'm gonna make you sorry little rat! You watch! You watch!"

He had the plan all worked out when he was chasing Fezzi in the park. The cul-de-sac was the best place to trap him, as Jabran predicted that Fezzi would never go into the house at the end of the street. That house from his dreams. But now things had not gone Jabran's way, and he was furious, as he wasn't used to this. He believed that he could do anything he wanted to people weaker than him and control what they did. But now his self-confidence was fading, and he was feeling rather uneasy, as if he felt the presence of something dark and bottomless. He had always been afraid of this ghastly house. It was one of the few things in the world which he didn't like thinking about, along with his dad, his absent mum and his miserable homelife. The house had given him nightmares in the past because he had seen too many horror movies about scary houses. Consequently, he hated this great building and even hated his mum and dad, because they made him feel weak, frightened and lonely. Deep inside, Jabran knew he had little control in his life, his bullying was wrong, and this scared him as he would have to face some uncomfortable truths about himself.

But also, when Jabran's dad stumbled home drunk, picking on him and slapping him around, Jabran felt miserable to his core. He didn't like being bullied by his dad, so he tried to distract himself by picking on other people, as it made him feel powerful. Now Jabran regretted that he had come down the cul-de-sac behind the park. Then, bellowing at the top of his voice, he gave his final threat:

"You listening you little rat? Think you've got away now do yer? Well, I'm gonna find you later on, just you wait, just you wait!"

Then he turned and began sprinting away.

3

Suddenly, a faint cry arose from somewhere in the house. Jabran heard it and halted. For a minute, he thought it was Fezzi's voice, so he listened for a while. The voice drifted along the breeze again and Jabran realised it was not Fezzi's voice. It sounded like a little girl and it was more like a long moan, or somebody sulking, rather than crying out. Jabran felt very strange inside. He somehow recognised that voice but didn't know how. The voice echoed again, this time much louder, and rather sinister as it was carried in the wind up to him. Jabran was sure he knew the voice but was kicking himself to establish where he had heard it. It was like something you had heard when you were small, or in one of those vivid dreams that you fail to remember, once you're awake.

Jabran had now completely forgotten about Fezzi. Incidentally, while Jabran had been waiting there, Fezzi had run around the house into the overgrown back garden, reached the back wall, climbed over and had sprinted away down the alley behind the garden, which came onto the main road.

Jabran couldn't move. That horrible moaning voice had gripped his soul and had moved him so much that he stood there, rooted, frozen. Inside, he was terrified. He was having flashbacks of his past nightmares of being inside the gigantic house, alone, walking up the stairs, which crumbled beneath his feet, falling into the cellar. Then he would hear his dad's angry voice coming closer and closer... Or he was running backwards and forwards but couldn't find a door to escape, or he was locked in a room upstairs, and the room was shrinking, and however hard he tried he couldn't push it back. Or he was in the hallway, rushing towards the front door, but however long he ran, the door always seemed far ahead. And sometimes, in his nightmares, he would just find himself in the corner beneath the stairs, moaning and crying...

Whenever he awoke, he felt deep hatred for the house, and his dad, because they kept scaring him and beating him, and there was nothing he could do about them, because they were too big and frightening, and he was so powerless. A desperate yearning would ache in his heart, to have a normal, loving family, like all the other children in his town. They were all so lucky to have kind and loving mothers and fathers, taking them to school, helping them with homework. And he was the only one with a rotten dad and a rotten life. This was why he had to make them all pay for the rotten time that he was having.

Jabran stood, entranced, gripped by the unmistakeable moaning, wondering whether he would remain frozen there, like a spooked statue, forever. Suddenly, as if the house pulled him forward, Jabran felt himself taking steps forwards, involuntarily. He couldn't help it. This voice had somehow bewitched him and was pulling him towards it. He hardly noticed himself opening and closing the screeching gate, walking up to the porch and noticing a massive, man-made hole in one of the boarded, bottom-floor windows, crawling in and then standing alone in this creepy old house. But the strong whiff of poo suddenly hit Jabran, and he realised he had stepped on something very stinky, like a skunk.

"Oh, POO!" He cursed to himself, while scraping his shoe against the skirting board. He must have stood there in that dark hallway for many seconds, scraping away the muck, when he finally realised where he was and let out a sudden shriek.

Jabran peered around and began shivering. Even the stench was now the last thing to worry about. Ahead of him was a spacious landing, leading to a grand staircase. To the left was a door leading into an adjacent room and the hallway carried on, patched with doors for several rooms it seemed. Jabran thought this was probably the biggest house he had ever been in. It was a whopper of a place! For a second, his trepidation was overcome with awe. But then, there it was again. The moaning. Clearer this time. It was coming from somewhere nearby, up the stairs or around the hallway. He listened carefully to locate the source. What struck Jabran after paying some attention was that this voice didn't sound human and this realisation made him tremble. Perhaps the stories of ghosts and goblins were true. Jabran was now shivering in the throes of terror, not knowing what to do, bewildered about why he had been so stupid to put himself in this situation. His imagination was bringing up the memory of a ghastly film called *The House*, which was about a man trapped in a dark house with zombies. *No!* He thought, *think of something funny*. He desperately worked to superimpose the images of the horror film with funny things like teddy bears and farting noises. That didn't help because he started imagining a farting teddy bear creeping up on him in the darkness! Jabran began looking around frantically. It wasn't pitch-dark in the hallway, but he felt as if any moment he could be caught and taken to a dungeon and be terrorised by an eggy teddy bear.

Then the voice echoed again. Very close this time. In fact, Jabran thought the voice seemed to come from somewhere below or behind the staircase and, to Jabran's surprise and terror, he could make out a door in the staircase. A cellar. But there was something different in the voice this time. He was beginning to recognise this moaning, which certainly wasn't human, as the voice was too rough and light to be a person. Then Jabran got it. *It must be an animal! Trapped under the stairs. A dog or even a cat!* Relief now spread through his veins, so much that now he felt more courage to do something. And he thought he didn't have to worry about lurking, putrid zombies or teddy bears farts, as the whining was probably coming from some stupid little, stray animal trapped in the cellar, which didn't matter. So, Jabran wiped his face, composed himself, shed all the silly thoughts and advanced towards the hole he had climbed through. Just then, he heard a string of voices, this time human ones, coming from outside, making their way in, all of them of older boys...

4

"Who are yer! Who are yer! Who are yer!"

"Where's our little toy, lads? Let's have some fun!"

"We're coming to the forbidden house boys! Wooooo! Beware of the little ghosties!"

These were the voices of bigger boys and this was probably their hang out, Jabran realised to his horror. Now any fears of smelly teddy bears in the darkness disappeared completely. This was a real-life threat. If they found Jabran, there was no telling what they would do. He wasn't really frightened of the older boys in the town, as none of them were as scary as his dad, but he never underestimated what a gang of them could do and he always avoided the older gangs on the street. Jabran was no fool. But now he was in an expanding quandary and he had to think fast to get himself out of it.

Jabran looked to and fro for a hiding place; the boys were now climbing through the hole in the board. Jabran tried opening the adjacent doors, but they were locked. He then crept down the hallway while the boys had suddenly stopped and began fooling around.

"He's a wimp! He won't come in!"

"Yes, I will, you idiot!"

"Come on then!"

In that instance, while this little argument erupted, Jabran found an open door; inside was a store cupboard, full of dusty cleaning materials and cobwebs, but it was deep enough to hide in. What was reassuring was that a natural gap in the door allowed Jabran to see what the boys were doing and if they were coming near to him. He watched, silent and nervous, as now the boys strolled into the hallway.

The biggest, meanest-looking lad kicked a

piece of debris recklessly, which went whizzing through the passage and hit Jabran's door. He winced.

"What a shot, lads! Right on target!" This was the boss, tall, lean, mean-looking, with scars from old fights shining proudly on his face. No one messed with him.

"So, what we gonna do today boss?" Asked a lanky boy who seemed to be the number two of the gang.

"How about dares?" Said one of them from behind, struggling to get a look in.

"Yeah!!!" A chorus of cheers roared out.

"Nah, there's no point doing dares, if not everyone is gonna take part, nudge, nudge, wink, wink," said the lanky number two, pointing at the punk who was afraid of coming in earlier.

"Oh, shut up you fool! I haven't seen you come in here alone," the so-called wimp retorted. Number Two glared at him.

"Okay lads, calm down, calm down, don't get your knickers in a twist. If we play dares, then he goes first," said the leader, pointing at his number two, which brought laughter and jeers from the rest.

"Anytime mate, I'm always up for it," boasted Number Two defiantly.

"Anyway, forget that boys, let's have another session with our little pet!" Once again, nasty jeering and shouting filled the dusty old house. Jabran noticed that, since the big boys had arrived, the moaning had ceased.

"It was sooo funny last time. We threw Kazza in the cellar and the dog nearly bit him! He was banging on the door and screaming, let me out! Let me out!" laughed the boss. Kazza, the reluctant one from earlier, went red with embarrassment and anger.

"Yeah," started Number Two, "but this kills it! Del had this gigantic water pistol, right, and he brought some dog food with him; he put some at the top and made the little mutt come up and then completely mashed it up with water! It was hilarious! The dog screamed like a ..."

"Like a dog?" added Del, a short, round, dim-witted bully.

"Yeah, yeah, like a total dog," laughed Number Two, unaware of the nonsense he just spoke. "Can we get that gun back?"

"Nah, we can't man," complained Del, "my brother took it back. He went schizo when he found out I took it."

Jabran had followed everything that had been said so far and was beginning to feel a hidden pain. Not a stomach ache, not a physical pain, but something frightening he had never felt before.

"Alright, let's get on with it then!" yelled the boss. "Open the door!"

The boys watched as Del undid the slide bolt lock on the cellar door and slowly opened it. Suddenly, a weak bark was heard. Jabran realised his guess had been correct. He shuddered. A dog was trapped in that cellar. A living creature had called out for help and had caught his attention. And the scary thing was this: Jabran knew in his heart of hearts, this was the voice he had heard before in his dreams...

5

Nervously, struggling inside, Jabran watched, as the boys peered down into the cellar, giggling and joking.

"Aw, you lot are tight, man!" said Kazza. "How can you let that thing stay down there and starve?" He sounded amused, but there was a hint of sincerity in his voice.

"Flippin mutts deserve it! Leaving all their poo on our streets. We're doing a community service!" proclaimed the boss.

"But what if the RSPCA find out or the police? Shouldn't we tell them? It might have an owner." Now Kazza was talking sense.

"Who gives a monkey? We're just havin a bit of fun. The mutt doesn't feel anything either way. We'll let it go after a while."

"Would you like it if someone trapped you in a cellar and threw things at you and teased you?" Now Kazza was becoming serious. The boss and the rest of the boys looked him up and down menacingly.

"What's wrong with this guy?" said the boss, sarcastically, side-glancing at the others. "He sounds like a stupid teacher."

"Yeah," added Number Two, grateful that the focus was not on him, "he'll give us a lecture on animal rights in a minute. Power to the ape, man!"

"I was just saying," Kazza immediately regretted showing his true colours to these lot and retreated into himself.

"Look, we didn't ask you to come with us, so if don't like the way we have some fun, you can get lost!" snarled the boss.

"Okay, that sounds a good idea." With that, Kazza stormed off.

"What an idiot!" yelled Number Two. "That guy needs a slap, man."

"We'll sort him out later, don't worry. And now boys, let the fun begin!" announced the boss and he produced some tennis balls from the plastic bag he was holding.

"Let's have some target practice. If you miss the mutt, you have to walk all the way up the stairs and to the end of the landing and back again. That's where the ghosts are..."

"Oh my god! That's dark!" The rest of gang replied, getting excited by the prospect of who would be the unlucky soul to walk up to what they thought was the haunted part of the house.

One by one, the boys began, quite violently, hurling the tennis balls at the dog down in the cellar. Every time the ball found its target, Jabran could hear a desperate cry of pain from the creature, which felt like a needle prodding into the undiscovered depths of his heart. And the boys applauded each other and swore each time the dog was hit.

"What a shot!"

"Wicked!"

"Did you hear it squeal? Stupid mutt!"

Jabran watched the cruel boys indulging in their game from the safety of his hiding place. Two waves were flowing up and down his heart and mind: anger and shame. Tears suddenly fell from his eyes, and he slumped against the wall of the cupboard because he couldn't watch anymore. He covered his eyes and his face. The pain the dog felt reminded him of his own pain. It didn't deserve to be imprisoned in this manner just as he didn't deserve to be bullied by his dad. In fact, and this was when the penny finally dropped into Jabran's mind and went swirling into the pits of his conscience. No one deserved to be treated this way. He realised that his dreams had given him some kind of a message or had led him here, to this place, to this moment, to this understanding. No human, no living being, no one deserved to be treated this way. He now thought of Fezzi and all the kids he had tortured over the years. He had trapped and taunted them. He had taken his anger out on them and he was trying to feel powerful. But did they deserve that? Should they have to pay for Jabran's unhappiness? Should he not find someone who could help him?

Now, for the first time, in many years, since his mother had left, Jabran released a flood of tears, which had been building up since his troubles began. The game continued; the boys cheered; the dog whimpered; and on and on Jabran wept.

The angry, surly, horrible, famously cruel, careless Jabran, Jabran the terrible, Jabran the mighty, Jabran the bully, was now sobbing silently, like a lonely infant on the playground.

In this house, at this moment, two souls had reached the lowest points of their lives, a stray dog and a bully boy. Their sadness merged; their cries intertwined and danced like a lost, melancholic fairy floating around, searching for home and rest.

6

Now, a few members of the gang had missed the poor creature and the fiendish game had halted.

"Right you lads, right up the stairs, down the landing and back!" ordered the boss.

This was no mean feat. It was dark and menacing on the first-floor landing, which was decorated with old, portrait paintings, which seem to stare out and smile. What made it worse was the creepy wallpaper on both sides; Victorian floral designs that looked like demonic faces.

Reluctantly and now grouping close together, the three loser boys edged up the stairs as the winners looked on, in delight. The boss followed from behind to ensure none of them cheated.

Jabran was now drying his tears and felt that something had really changed for him. He knew he had to get this dog out of the cellar and free it from its life of torture. He also felt a strange connection or sympathy to this animal, which had reached out to him in his dreams. Somehow, he could relate to it and see things from its point of view. But he had to be careful here. These boys were deadly. By the size of the boss, Jabran knew that these guys could seriously hurt him, so he decided to wait until this nasty lot left before he freed the dog.

Screaming, bellowing and laughter filled the air. Suddenly, a rush of almighty thudding footsteps swept through the house.

"O my days!!!"

"That was pure jokes!"

"I saw it! I saw it!"

The gang could be heard leaving the house, smacking each other on the back, proud of the jokes and dares they had given each other. The boys seemed to have caused an uproar in their dare. But what happened was that basically a gang member had hidden upstairs and jumped out in front of the losers, who screamed and went sprinting down the stairs. It all ended in jokes and laughter, which seem to disappear into the warm air outside.

Jabran listened intently. Moments elapsed. Nothing. They must have gone. Painstakingly, Jabran nudged the door open and peered once again into the corridor. Empty. The coast was clear. Without any hesitation, he flew up to the cellar door, which opened with a loud creak, and then he shone his mobile phone light downwards.

Two, large, crestfallen eyes looked back at him and Jabran recognised the head and body of a Labrador. It looked up as the light shone on its eyes, panting intermittently. It looked terribly weak and tired. Perhaps its legs were trapped. But Jabran was now determined to do something. Not just about this dog, but about his dad too. He would tell someone the truth and free himself, just like he was about to release this poor Labrador.

But Jabran was torn away from his thoughts by a tap on his shoulder. He turned. Facing him stood the towering, cruel face of the boss and behind him the menacing gang. They had crept back in after hearing the creaking door.

"Another toy to play with, Jabran," said the

boss, wickedly. And before Jabran could react, he saw the boss's strong hands shove him in the face, he toppled backwards and went crashing down the stairs...

7

Jabran felt warm breath and a bony body on his cheek. He right leg throbbed agonizingly, and he screamed in pain. He felt the floor for his phone, but to no avail. The pain flooded his leg again, as if it was being twisted into a knot. His tearful screams rose up the stairs and echoed. The dog followed suit and howled sympathetically. Above, weak rays of light streaked through the door which was ajar but there was no sign or sound of the gang.

"HELP!" bawled Jabran again, desperate and ridden with excruciating pain in his leg. He reached down gently to his right leg and felt it. His knee felt sore, but when he tried to straighten it, that's when the pain rocketed. He must have broken it, he thought. The Labrador only arched his head around and stared at Jabran in the darkness melancholically.

"HELP!" he screamed. He knew he was in trouble. Once more, he felt the ground for his phone but surmised those scumbags must have stolen it when he fell, or it might have fallen nearby and smashed to smithereens. He couldn't remember falling, only the sadistic eyes of the gang boss and his sniggering cretins.

Would he be trapped here forever with this poor dog and have tennis balls thrown at him for fun? Would he just lie here and wither away? No one knew he was here, except for the gang, and, judging from their behaviour, he knew they were going to make him suffer. The boss had recognised Jabran, probably from seeing him around the town. Jabran didn't hang around with the older boys, but most of them knew who he was. In fact, many of them kept their distance, owing to his size and mean father. But the boss knew him alright. And Jabran now realised that he was in for hell before they decided to let him go. If only he could just get up and make a run for it. But that was not going to happen. Jabran had badly injured his leg and was not going anywhere.

From feeling the refreshing tears of guilt, he

now felt desperation and anger flooding his eyes.

"HELP!" he cried, once more. This time he yelled with his whole being, releasing all the pain and regret in his soul. This impelled the dog to join him, and now both boy and canine howled a poignant duet in the darkness.

Then thud! Jabran's head fell to the floor. The room gyrated momentarily, and when Jabran came back to his senses, he realised the Labrador had got up. It was standing on all fours and panting!

"Good boy," gasped Jabran, pointing upwards. "Go and get help! Go on boy!"

This seemed to do the trick because the Labrador starting woofing enthusiastically and licked Jabran's leg softly, as if to soothe the pain. And funnily enough, it did seem to calm the ache for a while.

"Please boy, please," he urged, "go up, get help."

The dog just stood there, passively, and sniffed at Jabran's hurt leg.

"Please boy! Please!" he howled, as the pain shot through him again. "Please help."

His pleas just disappeared in the darkness and the Labrador just looked into Jabran's eyes, full of sympathy and understanding.

Then, as if by magic, the skinny Labrador let out a great woof, and scampered up the stairs like he was a born-again sheep dog! It turned to face Jabran, looking straight down at him, with a rather queer, intent look. This made Jabran smile and forget his leg. This creature had been through hell and now it stood there, free, reborn, with an invigorated spirit. And what made Jabran smile was that he had helped to free it from its prison. His tumble down the stairs must have released the Labrador's legs and it had probably just stood there, getting its feeling back. He had never helped anyone before. This was the first time in his whole life. The first time that he, the one who was the usual cause of pain and suffering, had helped to release another from such pain. This felt deeper, stronger and more powerful than the thrill of chasing Fezzi and stealing his lunch. Helping someone, especially for a wretched soul like Jabran, felt like drinking elixir from the fountain of God.

"Good boy!" Jabran yelled back. "Good boy!" And with that, the Labrador disappeared through the door and Jabran lay back in the darkness.

As he remained there, the pain excruciating, Jabran blacked out. Now, slipping out of consciousness, his whole boy fell dramatically, like he was plunging in a rollercoaster, his head spinning, his body tingling in awe. There, in the darkness, Jabran looked upon something slowly materialising, something illuminated, coming closer. He walked towards it. A bright light shone, and there stood the Labrador, its eyes beautifully deep and kind, its body now sleek and golden, ripples of joy moving around its frame. Jabran embraced it, felt its heart beating, heard each pulse like falling drops in a still pool. He sat and embraced this soul for hours. All of a sudden, its body shivered, Jabran let go. The Labrador had transformed into a familiar shape. Fezzi. Both boys stared at each other, surrounded by the darkness. Falling to his knees, Jabran wept. Fezzi also wept, as both boys remembered all the pain they had experienced. He looked up again. Fezzi was no longer there, but it was dog again. It gazed into Jabran sympathetically and then disappeared. At that moment, Jabran awoke, hearing adult voices above him.

8

Jabran's dad, Jabir, had a very odd experience. He was driving his odd job van around the town, snarling and sneering at other odd job men in their vans, puffing on his cigarette, when he heard a voice. He brought his vehicle to a screeching halt and parked on the side. Then, he arched around to look in the back. Just his tools and overalls. But the voice came clear again.

"HELP!" it screamed.

Someone was in trouble. Someone in the van. Someone he knew... It was as if the voice was inside his head as well as around it.

"HELP!" He heard it again. But this time the cigarette fell from his mouth. It was his son's voice, Jabran!

"Jabran!" he shouted. "Where the hell are you?" He got out of the van, checked the back again, did some circuits and then checked the back again.

"HELP!" Again.

"Jabran, you little devil. You watch when I catch you!" Jabir started thinking his son may be up to one of his tricks. "JABRAN!"

"Are you alright sir?" asked a policeman on patrol.

Jabir looked around, rather embarrassed. But before he could answer the policeman, he heard it again.

"HELP!" As clear as day.

Jabir glanced at the policeman, waiting to hear what he may say. He must have heard the voice.

"Well, are you alright sir?" He asked, looking plainly into Jabir's eyes, weighing up if there may be a crime transpiring.

"No, sorry, officer, I was just annoyed by something. It's fine." And he bid good day to the policeman and got back into his van.

What on earth was going on? Just before Jabir could start the engine, and continue with his work, suddenly, he saw the great, old house in the cul-de-sac, hovering before him, like a miniature movie screen in the air. He rubbed his eyes. He wasn't dreaming. He wasn't hallucinating. It was really there. Then he saw a door inside the house. Behind the door, he saw a Labrador gazing at him and he heard the desperate cry of his son, Jabran.

"HELP!"

"Jabran," he whispered, "you're in trouble..."

And, now, driven by the will to check his sanity and the deep dread that something was wrong, Jabir drove straight towards the cul-de-sac behind the park.

9

When Jabir arrived on the cul-de-sac, he found police cars, an ambulance and the neighbours gathering outside the old Lord's town house. He got out of the car and walked over to the gathering of locals, who were talking to a policewoman and pointing at the CCTV cameras hidden away in their bedroom windows.

Then Jabir's heart fell into a fissure, for he saw his son, Jabran, being taken away on a stretcher.

"Jabran! That's my son! Hey, wait a minute!"

Suddenly, the neighbours stopped whispering and stared at Jabir and the policewoman approached him.

"Don't worry, sir, don't worry. He's in good hands. This is your son then?"

Jabir presented his driver's licence and the policewoman showed it to the resting Jabran in the ambulance. She returned, smiling.

"Yes, your son hurt himself in that wretched house. We tried to get the council to board it up again because kids were getting in there. But they never listen. Anyway, the paramedics are just checking him over. I think he has broken his right leg," Jabir gasped, "but he should be okay," reassured the policewoman.

"Thank you, officer, thank you. What happened? Where did they find him?"

"Well, he must have fallen down into the cellar and, if it hadn't been for an anonymous call about a trapped Labrador, we would never have found him."

Jabir listened to the policewoman's story. He was perplexed and shocked by the vision he had seen. He feared about his sanity and then about his drinking habits and temper. Inwardly, he was afraid his son might not want his help; he hadn't been a very good father after all. In fact, the thought chimed in his head loud and clear; Jabran's voice seemed to have unblocked his senses; he had been a terrible father.

"You can accompany him to the hospital and we'll bring your van along if you want."

"Yes please, officer" answered Jabir, with uncharacteristic politeness.

Jabir stepped up onto the ambulance and entered. Lying there, gently smiling was his son Jabran. He seemed to have changed slightly, Jabir thought. The horrid arrogance, which he had inherited from his father, was no longer there. Instead, his son looked clearer, more innocent. He was only eleven years old. And now, after Jabir had heard his son's voice crying for help and had seen the face of that enigmatic Labrador, something softened inside him for his son. Maybe there was some good in him, and in himself, after all.

10

So, the news spread around the town like wildfire. Jabran, the meanest, cruellest, worst bully ever had broken his leg and was prancing around on crutches. And, to top if off, he was seen crying his eyes out in school!

The children viewed Jabran with an air of self-righteousness and justice. He got what he deserved, they thought. Some parents and teachers silently praised the skies for this victory over, who they saw, as one of the nasty boys of the town. Mrs Ali was sympathetic to Jabran's injuries and when the full story emerged, Jabran was seen in a totally different light.

One of the neighbours on the cul-de-sac had CCTV evidence of the gang entering and exiting the old house at the time Jabran had been injured. After some inquiries and hard questioning, it was revealed that Kazza had made the anonymous call to the police. Then all the knots began loosening. The gang ratted on the boss, who was charged with GBH and cruelty to animals and sent away to a young offenders' institution. The rest of the lads were forced to do community service, which involved helping the local council to clean up the old house and also helping to clear up dog's mess in the local shelter.

The mystery Labrador, however, was never found, despite the fact that the boys each described it and Jabran had also given his statement about it. But he did see it in his dreams sometimes. Jabran had come to respect his dreams and the places they may come from. The locals heard about the whole story and actually came to appreciate Jabran's actions with the Labrador.

Jabir, on the night his son was in hospital, got in contact with Jabran's mother, because he felt she should know what had happened. During the course of their conversation, he broke down, remembering the visions and the voice. He rarely spoke what was on his mind. And this time he did. His ex-wife listened, at first suspicious because she had dealt with his manipulations before, but then, the more he told her, the more she began to feel that something truly supernatural had occurred to Jabir.

It wasn't one of those perfect endings, they didn't get back together, but it was the beginning of repairing broken bridges and mum eventually felt safer interacting with Jabir and her son again. Jabir stopped the drinking, attended counselling sessions and found that his odd job business began picking up. What's more, he had a new apprentice who would accompany him for jobs on the weekend and the school holidays, Jabran!

And now Jabran was no longer the bully. The metamorphosis was complete. Now he was the protector of the weak and champion of the good! Fezzi, his erstwhile punch bag, was now his closest ally, and together, they worked on building a new platform game for Android apps, in which school children have to run away from a farting teddy bear that keeps yelling: "YOU WHAT! YOU WHAAT! YOU WHAAAT!"

And they called it Smelly Teddy!

ABOUT THE AUTHOR

Novid Shaid is an English teacher from the UK, who has taught in various secondary schools for over eighteen years. His first published work is the novel, *The Hidden Ones.* He shares short stories and poems on his website, www.novid.co.uk and his books can be found on Amazon.